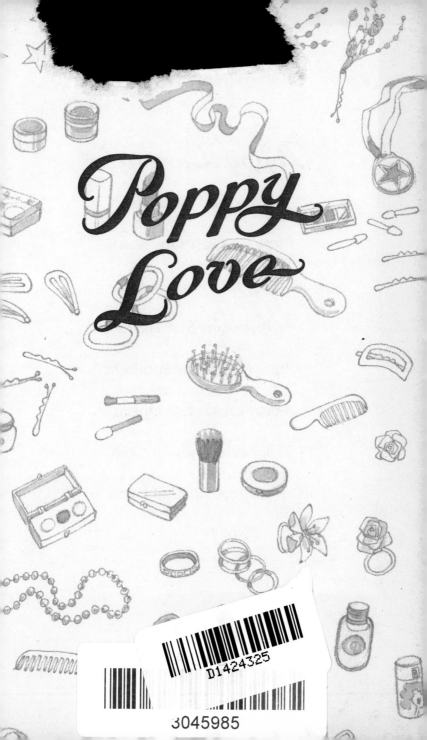

Poppy Love

Poppy Love titles

Poppy Love Steps Out

Poppy Love Faces the Music

Poppy Love Rock 'n' Roll

Poppy Love Star Turn

Poppy Love In the Spotlight

Poppy Love Tango Queen

Poppy Love Goes for Gold

Poppy Love All That Jazz!

Poppy Love

Dancing on Air

NATASHA MAY

illustrated by

SHELAGH MCNICHOLAS

WALKER
BOOKS

With thanks to Neil Kelly and the students of
Rubies Dance Centre
N.M.

With thanks to Carolyn, Julia, Kirsty and Ann at
Bell's Dance Centre
S.M.

This is a work of fiction. Names, characters, places and incidents are
either the product of the author's imagination or, if real, are used
fictitiously. All statements, activities, stunts, descriptions, information
and material of any other kind contained herein are included for
entertainment purposes only and should not be relied on for accuracy
or replicated as they may result in injury.

First published 2011 by Walker Books Ltd
87 Vauxhall Walk, London SE11 5HJ

2 4 6 8 10 9 7 5 3 1

Text © 2011 Veronica Bennett
Illustrations © 2011 Shelagh McNicholas

The author and illustrator have asserted their moral rights
in accordance with the Copyright, Designs and Patents Act 1988

This book has been typeset in ITC Giovanni

Printed and bound in Great Britain by Clays Ltd, St Ives plc

British Library Cataloguing in Publication Data:
a catalogue record for this book is available from the British Library

ISBN 978-1-4063-2911-7

www.walker.co.uk

Contents

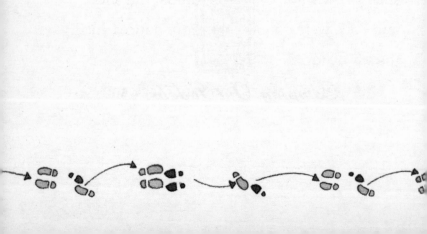

Fat Sam's Speakeasy

Poppy Love loved ballroom dancing.

She and her partner, Zack Bishop, had
dance classes with Miss Johnson every week
at the Blue Horizon Dance Studio. Poppy
especially liked doing Latin American dances,
such as the samba and the rumba, but she
and Zack were good at ballroom dances, like
the waltz, too.

One evening, after Poppy and Zack and

their friends had finished dance class, Poppy's Auntie Jill, who ran the Hotel Gemini with Poppy's mum, came to collect her. "Look at this!" she said, holding up a copy of *The Stage*.

"Do you mean the ad for the audition?" asked Nick. "Everyone at school's talking about it."

Nick was older than Poppy and attended Burne Hall, a full-time dance school. He danced with Emma Feltham, and their partnership was getting better and better.

"Well, it's a great opportunity," said Auntie Jill, folding back the pages to show a large

advertisement. "They're asking for dancers to audition for *Bugsy Malone*."

"That's a movie, isn't it?"

asked Poppy's friend Sophie. "With kids playing all the parts?"

"That's right," said Auntie Jill, "but it's a stage show too. It's a musical about American gangsters in the 1920s. They have splurge guns that spray people with white gooey stuff."

"Splurge guns!" cried Sophie's partner, Sam, pretending to "splurge" Luke and Zack, who dutifully fell over.

Miss Johnson came out of the studio. "Hello, Jill," she said, joining the children gathered round the newspaper.

"Hi, Sarah," said Auntie Jill. "Have you seen *The Stage* this week?"

"No, I don't usually buy it," replied Miss Johnson. "You all look very interested in something, though!"

"I think it might interest you, too," said Auntie Jill, handing Miss Johnson the newspaper.

Miss Johnson began to read. "This sounds great!" she said. "A professional show, and it's going to be on here, in Brighton, for a pre-West End run."

"Professional means you get paid, doesn't it?" asked Sam.

"Yes," said Miss Johnson.

"What's a pre-West End run?" asked Zack.

"It means that the show will start in Brighton but transfer to a theatre in London after a few weeks," explained their teacher, still reading. "It starts in November," she went on.

"They need actors, singers and dancers aged from ten to fourteen."

"Wow!" beamed Luke's partner, Cora. "I'd love to be in a show. Wouldn't you, Poppy?"

Poppy had been listening with interest, but something was puzzling her. "Yes, I would," she replied. "But we do *ballroom* dancing. There isn't any ballroom dancing in *Bugsy Malone*, is there?"

"You're right, Poppy," said Miss Johnson. "There won't be any quicksteps or tangos. But they'll need dancers who can work well together in couples, or in a chorus line, and pick up steps quickly. And ballroom dancers are pretty good at that, aren't they?"

Poppy thought about last summer. She and Zack had gone to a dance summer school and tried different kinds of dancing – ballet, tap and jazz. Poppy really liked jazz, an American style of show dance that was such fun to do, it made her feel like the star of a high school musical!

She also thought about the formation dance she and the others had done in last year's Christmas show, and the samba they'd presented at a dance festival last summer. The dancers had to do all their steps exactly in time with each other, using the same foot, with their arms in the same position. It took practice, but it looked great when they got it right. "We *are* good at that!" she agreed.

"So who'd like to audition?" Miss Johnson asked the children.

Almost everyone put up their hand.

"I thought so!" said Miss Johnson. "Ask your parents, and then we'll see." She thought for a moment. "It would be great publicity for the Blue Horizon, wouldn't it?"

"Yes!" answered the children.

"As long as it doesn't interfere with your school work too much," she added.

"No!" they chorused, "it won't!"

Miss Johnson and Auntie Jill smiled at each other. "Thanks for bringing this in, Jill," said Miss Johnson. She turned to the children. "Let's go for it, then!" she said.

The audition was held in a rehearsal studio, a big empty room with a wooden floor. A mirror covered one wall, and a piano stood in the corner. A man whose name tag said

"Gary", and a woman who had "Teresa" on hers, sat behind a table at the front, ready to take notes as they watched the audition.

A thin man in black sweatpants and ballet shoes was jogging on the spot. "Come along, ladies!" he called as Poppy's group of twenty girls came in. "Find a place and let's warm up!"

Judging by the length of the line outside, hundreds of children were auditioning today. It was already four o'clock and the boys hadn't started yet. Poppy felt as if she had stepped into a new world, far away from her familiar one of ballroom competitions. There were so many talented

children here from all over the South East of England. They made Poppy feel like a very small poppy in a *very* large field!

"My name's Steve and I'll be teaching your class today," announced the thin man, still jogging. "Don't take any notice of these two sitting at the table, they're only Gary, the director, and Teresa, the choreographer!"

Gary and Teresa smiled, and some of the girls giggled nervously. Poppy knew that the director of the show was the most important person of all. The choreographer made up the dance routines, so she had an important job too. They would both be watching the dancers very closely. Steve was trying to make the children feel at ease, but Poppy was still nervous.

"It's 1929 and we're in New York, at Fat Sam's Grand Slam Speakeasy," said Steve, coming to a standstill and facing the mirror. The pianist played the music for the song "Fat Sam's Grand Slam", and Steve began to move his feet. "All around us are girls, guys, guns and gangsters," he went on. "Let your imagination take you there while you dance, and you'll be great. Now, follow what I do."

They began the warm-up exercises. Poppy felt better once she started moving, though the number pinned to her back and front was 13 – an unlucky number sometimes.

"Right!" called Steve after the warm-up. "Copy me!"

He began to dance the Charleston. Poppy and Zack's class had once done the Charleston, which was danced in couples,

as part of a quickstep
routine. You had to
swivel your feet and
kick out sideways
from your knee. At the
same time you had to cross your
hands backwards and forwards, like scissors,
or hold them out and roll them round and
round. "As if you're polishing an invisible
window," Miss Johnson had described it.

Poppy immediately began to copy Steve,
putting lots of energy into swivelling and
kicking on the beat of the music.
Other girls, who hadn't
done the dance before,
were slower to start, but
soon everyone was doing
the Charleston happily.

"Now, in a line, please!" instructed Steve.

The girls lined up across the room. Steve taught them a simple tap routine, allowed them to practise it a few times, then asked them to do it all together behind him, looking in the mirror. The girls had been asked to wear soft shoes for the audition, so there wasn't any tapping, but Poppy could tell the line was doing the sort of steps the chorus line at Fat Sam's would do. It looked good.

"Lovely, ladies!" encouraged Steve. "Let's do it again!"

After the tap dance they had a short rest, then Steve showed the girls a sequence of jazz steps. "Remember," he told them, "the 1920s was the age of jazz!"

Poppy put everything she could into the jazz routine. She remembered what the summer school teacher had told her about using her whole body, stretching even the parts that didn't seem important, like her neck, fingers and toes. With every step she tried to stretch just that little bit further, backwards, sideways, up towards the ceiling and down towards the floor, hoping that the director and the choreographer would like how she moved.

"Thank you, ladies!" said Steve, and he, Gary and Teresa applauded. "Recall will be on Thursday!"

With that, the audition was over. While Miss Johnson was unpinning Poppy's number, Poppy asked her, "What's recall?"

"It's when they ask the ones they like best to come back and dance again," said Miss Johnson.

The first boys' group was going in. Zack was number 8. "Good luck, Zack!" called Poppy and Miss Johnson.

"So if I don't get asked to come back on Thursday," said Poppy, "it means I'm not in the show. And if I do, it means I *might* be in it."

"Exactly," said Miss Johnson. "But listen, Poppy. Don't get your hopes up too much, will you? There are so many children here, and there are only a few parts for girls in this show."

Poppy nodded. "It almost makes me wish I was a boy," she said. "But not quite!"

Poppy couldn't believe it when she, Zack, Emma and Nick all got recalled.

"Isn't it amazing?" she said to Zack when they arrived at the recall audition on Thursday evening.

"No, it's not," declared Zack.

"But there were lots of really good dancers there!" protested Poppy.

"Yes," replied Zack, "including *us!*"

Poppy wished she could be as confident

as her partner. But she needn't have worried. She quickly found that she and Zack and Emma could do everything the other children could do. Nick and Amelia, a girl his age who went to his school, were auditioned separately, with the older girls and boys.

"I'm glad I'm not in competition with Amelia," Poppy confided to Zack during the break. "She's so good!"

Zack grinned. "We *are* in competition with this lot, though!" he said.

"And I think you're enjoying it!" laughed Poppy.

"Well, aren't *you*?" replied Zack.

Poppy looked round the studio at the boys and girls in their practice clothes, sitting and standing in groups, drinking from their water bottles and chatting to each other. Even though auditioning was nerve-wracking, she knew that this was definitely where she wanted to be. "Yes, I *am* enjoying it," she agreed.

At the end of the audition, Steve called all the dancers in and lined them up. "When I call your name, step forward," he said.

"Oo-er," whispered Zack. "I've seen this on telly. It's scary."

"Why?" asked Poppy, but Zack couldn't reply. Steve had started to read out names.

He did the older dancers first. Amelia remained in her place as the girls on each side of her stepped forward. She couldn't hide her disappointment, and Poppy felt sorry for her.

When it came to the older boys, Steve didn't call Nick's name. But Nick didn't look disappointed as he waited in the back line. Poppy thought his eyes looked as bright as her puppy Lucky's when he was waiting for her to throw his ball!

When Steve started on the younger children, Poppy's fingers and toes began to tingle as she listened hard for her name. Steve didn't say it. She couldn't look at Emma and Zack, especially when their names weren't read out either.

"Those of you in the back line," said Steve, "stay where you are. Those in the front line, thank you very much. You're free to go."

Poppy didn't understand. Did he mean the dancers he'd called out were the ones they *didn't* want?

She looked at the faces of the boys and girls Steve had asked to stay. They were all smiling.

"You never know which way round it's going to be," Nick told her. "But I thought we'd be OK!"

"Congratulations, ladies and gentlemen," said Steve, "and welcome to the cast of *Bugsy*. Contracts will be in the post tomorrow."

When he'd gone, Emma hugged Poppy. "Contracts!" she exclaimed. "That means we're real professionals. Isn't it exciting?"

Poppy's legs felt funny, as if they were having trouble holding her up. She remembered her words to Miss Johnson after the first audition. "Do you know something, Emma?" she asked with a wide smile. "I really like being a girl, but just this once, I wish I was a boy."

Emma was mystified. "Why?" she asked.

"I'd love to be a gangster in the show," said Poppy. "It would be so cool to get someone with a splurge gun!"

Stepping Stones

"I'm so tired!" Poppy said to Zack one Sunday afternoon, when they had practised their routines so many times she'd lost count. The rehearsals for *Bugsy Malone* were exciting, but very hard work.

"Me too," agreed Zack. "And I haven't even *looked* at my homework yet!"

Zack was a year older than Poppy and had just started at secondary school. Poppy knew that he was very determined, and would do everything he could to continue dancing as well as fitting in all the new things in his life. But he did look tired.

"Once the show starts, it'll be better," encouraged Poppy. "We're not in every performance, after all."

The rules about children performing on the professional stage meant that each child was allowed to do only a few performances a week. Each part was learnt by several children and shared between them.

"That's true," said Zack. He looked at Poppy eagerly, his tiredness forgotten. "Won't it be great to be professional dancers for two weeks, in a proper theatre, with a paying audience, and our names in the programme?"

He was wearing such a big smile, Poppy

couldn't help laughing. "You never know, it might be for longer than two weeks if we get chosen to go to London," she reminded him. "Wouldn't *that* be great!"

Zack's only reply was to do a silly little dance on the spot, which made Poppy laugh even more.

"What's the joke?" asked Dad, who had just arrived to collect them. "Can I join in?"

"If you like," said Zack mischievously. "Do what I do, Mr Love – that'll give us a laugh!"

So Poppy's dad copied Zack's silly dance, and then Poppy joined in, and they laughed so much in the car on the way home that they didn't stop until they dropped Zack off at his house.

"Bye!" called Poppy as Zack opened the car door.

Zack yawned. "I need to go to sleep, I think," he said, getting out of the car.

"Me too," said Poppy.

Zack made a face. "But I've got to do my homework," he said. He waved solemnly as he went in the front door, and Poppy waved back.

"It's a good job you haven't got homework at the moment, Poppy," said Dad, starting to drive away. "I hope Zack's managing to keep up at school."

"I think he is," said Poppy. "He always works hard, at everything."

Dad nodded. "If he wants to go on with this stage business, though," he said, "he'll have to work twice as hard."

Poppy was silent. She didn't know what to say. Did Dad mean that when *she* went

to secondary school next year, she'd have to work twice as hard as well?

"Child actors sometimes have teachers who come to the theatre, or the film studios, so that they don't have to go to school," said Dad.

"That sounds cool!" said Poppy.

Dad looked thoughtful. "Maybe," he said. "Schoolwork always comes first, you know, Poppy."

Poppy *did* know. Her older brother, Tom, was in his bedroom every evening, bent over his desk. And Poppy was busy enough *without* homework. This year, she couldn't be in the school pantomine, or Miss Johnson's Christmas show, because *Bugsy Malone* was on in November and December. And she and Zack and Nick and Emma and all the others were still doing their classes at the Blue Horizon. There were hardly enough hours in the day to fit everything in!

"I still want to be a dancer," Poppy said to Dad. "Like Auntie Jill used to be."

Dad parked the car outside the hotel, undid his seat belt and looked at her kindly. Poppy knew he understood how she felt about dancing. "I know, love," he said. "We'll just have to wait and see."

It was the first night of the show. The weeks since the audition had been so busy that they'd zipped by, and now Poppy and Zack were waiting in the wings with ten other children. They stood in a line, boys behind, girls in front, listening for the music that meant "you're on!"

Poppy had
never been
so excited, or
nervous, in her
life. Even though
she and Zack had
danced in important ballroom competitions,
this was *so* different. They wouldn't be
dancing on an empty floor but on a stage, set
up to look like Fat Sam's Speakeasy in New
York in 1929. Gary had explained that there
was a law in America at that time forbidding
the sale of alcoholic drinks, like wine, beer
or whisky. But people liked these drinks,
and thought of ways to get them anyway.
A speakeasy was a secret bar, where they
only let you in if you could "speak" the right
words at the hidden door.

There were tables and chairs, and a band, and actors being customers and waiters, and spotlights following the main characters. It wasn't just dancing, it was being part of a story.

The biggest difference, though, was that everyone was paid to work in show business. It was their job, just like Dad's job in London and Mum's at the hotel. Poppy's beautiful yellow dress, fringed with black, had been designed by a costume designer and made in the wardrobe department, along with her headdress of feathers. Her black dancing shoes had come from a special stage shop, and her hair and make-up had been done by a hairdresser and a make-up artist, instead of by Mum or Auntie Jill. It all made Poppy feel very special.

The music for "Fat Sam's Grand Slam" started. The singers began, Zack's grip on Poppy's hand got tighter and they bounded onto the stage.

At the dress rehearsal, the small audience was made up of people who worked on the show, as well as friends and relatives. But now, the theatre was filled with a huge number of faces, all looking at Poppy and the other dancers as they swivelled their feet and kicked their legs in the Charleston.

Poppy realized she was holding her breath, and tried to relax and enjoy herself. It was very hot under the stage lights, but they made the girls' dresses shimmer brightly as they danced, and showed up their

1920s-style red lipstick and thin, painted-on eyebrows. Zack and the other boys had had their hair slicked down with gel, as that was the fashion for men in the 1920s, and they wore black shoes with white tops. At the end of the dance, the noise of the applause was so loud, Poppy was thrilled!

"I can't wait to go on again!" she whispered to Zack when they came off.

"Me too," he agreed. Their next number was called "Show Business". They danced while the girl playing a character called Lena Marelli sang a song. "This is the *best*, isn't it, Pop!"

Zack's mum and Poppy's parents were in the audience tonight, and Auntie Jill and Uncle Simon would be there for Poppy's next performance. The first night was special

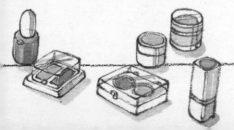

because it was the Press Preview, when the reviewers from newspapers saw the show and wrote about it the next day. Everyone would be very anxious tomorrow, waiting for the reviews to come out!

The children weren't allowed to watch from the wings, but Poppy didn't mind, as she'd seen it all during rehearsals. She thought the actors and singers, some of whom were only her age, were astonishingly good at their parts. Poppy was sure that if she had to sing alone, in front of all those people, she'd be too scared to open her mouth. But the boy playing Fat Sam, who had to wear a padded costume because he wasn't really very fat, and the girl playing Blousey Brown sang confidently.

Most of all, though, Poppy admired Amelia, who sat next to her in the dressing-room. She played Tallulah, Fat Sam's girlfriend. Poppy thought she was not only brilliant at acting, singing and dancing, but that she looked perfect in her 1920s-style costume, with her hair waved and her make-up on. It was hard to believe that she was a schoolgirl!

"I wish the show was on for longer than two weeks," Poppy said to Amelia as they waited in the dressing-room.

Amelia agreed. "And I wish they'd let us all do every performance," she said with a sigh. "I'd love to be here every night."

"If you get chosen to go to London," said Poppy, "will you do it?"

"You bet!" Amelia almost jumped out of her chair in excitement. "Imagine, dancing in a West End show!"

Poppy had been to the West End of London a couple of times to see shows in one of the many theatres there. The streets were crowded with people and traffic. But after dark, the area turned into a very special place. There were coloured lights everywhere, shining from advertisements, signs and streetlamps. They sparkled in the trees and on the bridges over the river Thames. Tall buildings, lit with floodlights, made beautiful reflections in the water.

"It would be great," Poppy said to Amelia, "but wouldn't you have to live in London?"

"Nick and I board at Burne Hall," said Amelia. "It's halfway between London and Brighton, so we can get to either one easily."

London was fifty miles from Brighton. Twenty-five miles was quite a long way to travel, do a show and get home again, but fifty miles was impossible.

"You're lucky," said Poppy.

After the show, Poppy and Zack met their families in the lobby. "Well done, Poppy!" said Dad, hugging her.

"You were all great, and we did enjoy the show, didn't we?" said Mum, turning to Mrs Bishop.

Mrs Bishop nodded. "Wasn't that girl who played Tallulah fantastic?" she said.

"Her name's Amelia," said Poppy, feeling important. "She sits next to me backstage."

Also in the lobby were several of the newspaper reviewers, talking to the director and the choreographer. Poppy and her family were just about to leave when Gary beckoned to Poppy and Zack.

"This is Bob Stillman," he said, indicating the man he'd been talking to, "from Southern TV. He'd like to have a word with you and your parents. Bob, meet Poppy and Zack."

Mr Stillman was young and cheerful-looking. "Great show," he said to the children. Then he turned to Poppy's parents and Mrs Bishop. "We'd like some of the cast to do a piece from the show for tomorrow evening.

Gary tells me Poppy and Zack aren't dancing tomorrow night." He turned back to the children, smiling. "So we thought perhaps you two and some other couples could do the Charleston number for us. How about it?"

Dancing on TV? Poppy couldn't believe what she was hearing! She and Zack had won competitions, and now they'd danced on the professional stage. Once they'd had an article written about them in the local paper. But they'd never been on TV before!

She and Zack looked at each other. "Wow, Pop!" said Zack.

"It's the local news programme," Mr Stillman was saying. "About half past six in the evening. We'd need you to be there a lot earlier, though, so it'll mean an afternoon off school."

Poppy crossed her fingers as Mum and Dad and Mrs Bishop exchanged looks. Please, please, *please* don't let them say no, she chanted silently.

"I don't see why not," said Mrs Bishop, watching Poppy's and Zack's faces. "It's only a couple of hours, and Wednesday afternoon is Games, isn't it, Zack?"

Zack grinned. "Thanks, Mum!" he said.

"What about me?" Poppy asked her parents.

"Well..." said Dad, looking serious.

"Just this once?" pleaded Poppy.

Dad began to smile. "OK, as it's only a couple of hours," he said. "Just this once, mind."

"Yay!" cried Poppy, jumping up and down.

While Mr Stillman spoke to the grown-ups about the arrangements for the next day, Zack and Poppy sat down on the thickly carpeted theatre stairs. "You know," said Zack, "now that we've been asked to dance on TV, it's like we're treading on the next stepping stone."

Poppy knew what he meant. "I wonder," she said, "where the stepping stone will lead us?"

Zack shrugged happily. "I don't know, Pop," he said, "but I can't wait to find out!"

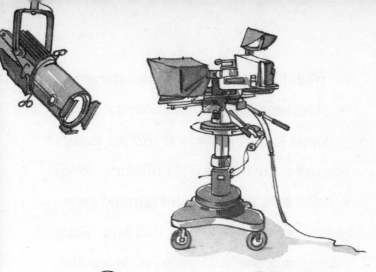

Dancing on Air

The stage lights were bright, but the television lights were even brighter.

"I wish they hadn't put so much make-up on us," grumbled Zack. "I feel kind of … orange."

Poppy was wearing more make-up than usual too, but she didn't mind. "Everyone wears make-up on TV," she said. "Even the prime minister."

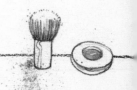

"Well, I bet he doesn't look as orange as me," insisted Zack.

Poppy knew Zack was as thrilled as she was to be dancing on TV, but when he was nervous he always got a bit grumpy. "It's because of the lights," she told him. "Auntie Jill says that bright TV lights make people's faces all pale and flat without make-up. When we get home we can watch the recording, and you'll see you look perfectly OK."

"I hope so," he said. "My mum will keep that recording for a hundred years. She'll still be showing it to people when I'm older than she is now."

"Oh, Zack!" laughed Poppy. "It'll be fun!"

Zack smiled. He never stayed grumpy for long.

"Right, kids, are you ready?" asked

Mr Stillman, who was wearing headphones and carrying a clipboard. "Time to go to the studio. You're on in two minutes."

They followed him to the studio door. Above it were the words ON AIR in red lights.

"Look," said Poppy, pointing to the sign. "I'm so happy that I really *am* dancing on air!"

The children giggled, and even Mr Stillman couldn't help smiling. "Quiet, now," he reminded them as they went in.

The studio wasn't very big. There was just room for a desk in front of some screens,

where the newsreader sat, and another screen
for the weather reporter. The ceiling was
hidden by the bright lights. Behind a glass
panel in one wall sat the people who put the
programme together. They were watching
what each camera was showing, working the
lights and the sound, and telling the people
down on the studio "floor", as Mr Stillman
called it, what was happening. Poppy had
often seen presenters on TV with earpieces
in their ears. Now she knew who was talking
to them!

In the corner was a space for the children to dance. When Poppy had seen it during the first run-through that afternoon, she'd understood why Mr Stillman wanted only three couples. The space was much smaller than the stage. So small, in fact, they'd had to change the routine a little bit to fit it in.

Poppy began to feel very excited as the dancers took up their positions. All around, cameras watched them like large animals prowling in a circle, and thick electric cables snaked across the floor. The lights were so strong that Poppy could feel their heat on her skin. Mum and Mrs Bishop and the other children's mothers would be watching on the screen in the "green room", as the waiting room backstage was called, while Dad and Tom and Auntie Jill and Uncle Simon and thousands and thousands of people Poppy didn't know would be watching on TV at home. It was a bit scary.

The newsreader introduced them, the music began and suddenly there was no turning back. They were dancing on TV – live!

"Don't look at the cameras," Mr Stillman had told them at rehearsal, "and *smile*!"

It was different from being on the stage, and more like they were dancing in the studio at the Blue Horizon. Poppy calmed her nerves by imagining just that, while she and Zack and the other two couples danced – and acted – just like they did on stage, pretending to be in Fat Sam's Speakeasy even though the stage set wasn't there.

Poppy hoped the Charleston looked as good as it felt. The trick was to make your limbs look loose, though you were in fact controlling them. "Carefree, bouncy, as if life's an endless party, that's the 1920s!" Teresa, the choreographer, had told them. Poppy let the Charleston music take her to that endless party.

She danced her heart out!

When they finished they were applauded by the presenters and crew in the studio.

Poppy felt very hot but very happy as Mr Stillman took them out of the studio and back to the green room.

"Fabulous!" said Mum, hugging Poppy.

"Did I look orange?" asked Zack.

"Not at all," said his mum. She didn't hug him. Since Zack had been at secondary school, he didn't think it was very cool to be hugged. "You looked fantastic. And you all danced so well!" she added, looking round at all six children's smiling faces. "What a great experience!"

Everyone was talking at once, congratulating one another and being embraced by their parents, when one of the girls from the wardrobe department came in. "Time to get changed," she said. "Show's over!"

"It's sad in a way," said Emma as they followed the girl down the corridor. "All that preparation for such a short performance."

"But the show's not really over," Poppy pointed out. "We get to do it three times a week for the next two weeks at the theatre."

"And," added Adam, Emma's partner, "if people liked what they saw tonight, they might book tickets for the show, and it'll be a huge success, and then who knows *what'll* happen!"

Who knows, thought Poppy, sitting down at the dressing-table and looking at herself in the mirror. Who knows?

Adam was right about people seeing the children's TV appearance and buying tickets for the show. The theatre was full every night, especially since the newspaper reviews had said that the

show was perfect entertainment for families. Poppy was very proud that she had been part of making *Bugsy Malone* such a success.

"Do you realize," said Zack as Mum dropped them off for Friday night's performance, "we finish a week tomorrow? It seems like we've only just started!"

"A show like this should be on at Christmas," Mum pointed out, "when people take children to the theatre."

"It *is* on at Christmas," said Poppy, suddenly feeling a little sad. "In London."

"Oh, of course!" remembered Mum.

Poppy hoped her parents would take her to see the show at Christmas in the West End. However many times she saw it, she never got tired of it. She knew that long after next Saturday, she would still hum the songs and do the dances in front of her bedroom mirror.

"Gary's going to let us know tonight which of us they want for the show in London," Poppy told her mum. "Maybe he'll make us line up and call out names, like he did at the audition."

Zack groaned. "I hope not. That was *scary*!"

After the show, Gary called everyone onto the stage, but he didn't call out any names. "Good news," he said, looking round at their expectant faces. "I'm glad to say that we've decided to offer London contracts to all of you."

He had to stop then because a huge cheer went up. But when everyone had stopped whooping and hugging each other, he began to give out forms.

"Ask your parents to fill these in," he said, "and bring them back by next Saturday, our last night here. We need to find out which of you will be able to come to London. And congratulations, everybody!"

Poppy looked at the form. She skipped the part about contracts and payments, but she read the bit at the bottom with a sinking heart. It said that each child had to have somewhere in London to stay before rehearsals could begin.

"My grandma lives in London," said Emma happily. "I'm sure she'll let me stay with her."

Zack looked at Poppy gloomily. Neither of them had relatives in London. "How much does a hotel cost?" he asked.

Poppy knew that staying in a London

hotel, for several nights a week for eight weeks, would be far more than their families could afford. "Too much," she replied.

"I could ask around at school," suggested Amelia. "Perhaps you could stay with someone's parents. We'd have to find somewhere else for Zack, though."

Poppy shook her head. "Thank you so much!" she said. "But Zack goes wherever I go."

Amelia giggled. "It's like you're stuck to each other!" she said, looking from Poppy to Zack and back again. "I bet you'll find a way to come to London."

"I'm not so sure," said Zack.

"You never know," said Amelia sympathetically. "Suppose something unexpected happens?"

The very next morning, something unexpected *did* happen.

Auntie Jill had brought Lucky, Poppy's puppy, over to play. Lucky lived with Auntie Jill and Uncle Simon because the Loves couldn't keep him in their flat at the top of the hotel. He was growing fast, and the bigger he got, the more Poppy loved him.

"Oh, Lucky, I wish we had a garden for you to run in!" she said, rolling his ball across the living-room floor for about the hundredth time that morning. He never seemed to get tired of bringing it back, his little tail wagging, and was always ready for another game.

Mum came in with a tray of drinks, followed by Tom and Dad. Lucky jumped up at Tom.

"Whoa, Lucky!" cried Tom, throwing the ball. "Here, fetch!"

Mum gave Poppy a glass of orange juice and sat down in the armchair. She knew Poppy was disappointed that she and Zack couldn't go to London. "I think it's about time we told you our big news, Poppy," she said. She looked at Dad, who nodded. Tom just grinned.

Mum took a deep breath. "We're going to sell the hotel to Auntie Jill and Uncle Simon," she said, "and move into a house."

Poppy almost dropped her glass in astonishment. "A proper house, with a garden?" she asked. "Where Lucky can play? Really and truly and really and truly?"

Dad laughed. "Two reallys and two trulys!" he teased. "But the main thing, Poppy," he went on more seriously, "is that we're going to move nearer to London. I'm so fed up with that journey!"

Poppy wasn't surprised to hear this. Most nights after work, Dad fell asleep in front of the TV.

"You're not getting any younger, after all, Dad!" joked Tom.

"Cheeky!" said Dad.

Poppy thought of something. "Does it mean we'll be going to new schools next year?" she asked.

Mum nodded. "Yes, it does," she said.

"Oh, Tom!" said Poppy. "I've got to go to a new school next year anyway, but won't you be sad to leave your school?"

Tom considered for a moment. "Yes and no," he said. "I don't want to leave my mates, but I'll make new ones."

Poppy knew he would. Tom was a naturally cheerful boy, never downcast for long. "Mum and Dad told me last week," he added. "It was really hard keeping it secret!"

"We didn't want to distract you from the show," explained Mum, "so we waited to see if you and Zack had been chosen to go to London before we told you. And tonight, all of us – Zack and his mum as well – are going to eat out at Uncle Simon's restaurant. To celebrate."

"Cool!" cried Poppy. But suddenly a thought came to her, like a thunderbolt. She felt hot, then cold again. "Er ... I'll still be able to come to Miss Johnson's classes when we've moved house, won't I?" she asked.

Dad shook his head. "Sorry, love," he said, "but we're going to be living too far away."

"Oh no!" exclaimed Poppy. "We can't go! I don't want to!" She tried not to cry, but couldn't help it. How could a piece of news be so wonderful and so horrible at the same time?

Mum put her arm around Poppy's shoulders. "Of course you feel like this now," she said, "but things change, you know, and often for the better."

"But this isn't better!" insisted Poppy. "It's worse! It's bad enough that Zack and I can't go to London, but now we won't be able to dance together at all!"

"You'll go to another dance school, though..." began Mum.

"No, I won't!" said Poppy.

"Calm down, love," said Mum, wiping Poppy's tears with a tissue. "Everything'll work out, you'll see."

Poppy felt awful. She couldn't pretend she was happy about moving when she wasn't.

Suddenly, she remembered Amelia's words. "I can't leave Zack," she told her mum. "I'm going to dance with him for ever and ever, because ... because I'm stuck to him!"

Camping Out Indoors

Poppy and Zack were dancing that afternoon in the Saturday matinée.

"Guess what?" Poppy blurted out to Zack as soon as she saw him at the theatre. "We've got to move away from Brighton. And I won't be able to come to Miss Johnson's any more!"

To her surprise, Zack already knew. "My mum told me," he said.

"Isn't it terrible!" said Poppy. "We've got to do something about it!"

Zack stopped at the door to the boys' dressing room. "Like what?" he asked.

Poppy shrugged. "I don't know, I could refuse to go to school," she suggested. "Or you could refuse to do your homework until they gave in."

"What good would that do?" asked Zack. "We'd just get into trouble at school, and your parents would still want to move."

Poppy knew he was right. But she thought about all the places she and Zack had been, and all the things they'd done, and the competitions they'd won, and she felt very sad. "Oh, Zack," she said, "I just can't believe we won't be dancing together next year!"

Zack didn't open the dressing room door.

He put his bag down and drew Poppy to the side of the corridor, so they wouldn't get in people's way. "Listen, Pop," he said. "I've got something to tell you."

Poppy could see he was serious. "What is it?" she asked.

"Well, I was already thinking I might have to stop dancing next year," said Zack, "or at least not do so much. School work takes up a lot of time. So maybe it's best that you'll be with a new partner after all."

Poppy didn't understand. "But *you're* my partner," she said, "and you always will be, won't you?"

He shook his head. "No, I won't," he said. "You'll make loads of new friends, and find another partner I suppose..." He stopped and thought for a moment, his serious look almost turning into a smile, as if his face didn't quite know what to do. "I suppose I will too, if I decide to carry on dancing. Things just change, don't they?"

Poppy thought about Tom, who played football only on Saturday afternoons now, instead of three times a week. Maybe things did just change, for all of them.

"All right," she said, though she wasn't sure she believed it. "But I'd still rather dance with *you*."

"You will," said Zack, "for the rest of this year. We've got tests and competitions, and I'm not going to let you down, am I?"

Poppy knew he wouldn't. He was being very grown up about everything. But although she was a year younger, she could be grown up too. "Maybe I'll see you at dance events," she said. "I mean, we're not moving that far away, are we?"

Zack's smile got as big as it could be. "You're the best, Pop!" he said.

Poppy loved eating at Uncle Simon's restaurant, Forrester's, especially on a busy Saturday night. She liked watching the waiters scurrying in and out of the swing doors from the kitchen, bringing trays of steaming hot food, while the bartender in his white jacket poured drinks. A young woman called Vanessa, looking very elegant in a black dress, welcomed people, showed them to their table and gave them menus. Uncle Simon seemed to be everywhere at once, making sure every diner was happy. But he always had time to join Auntie Jill and Poppy's family for a few minutes.

"Jill and I really enjoyed the show the other night," he told Poppy, taking her plate from the waiter's tray and setting it in front of her. "I thought it was brilliant."

Auntie Jill laughed. "For *you* to go to a musical," she teased Uncle Simon, "it must have been good!"

Uncle Simon looked sheepish. "Well, I couldn't miss seeing Poppy and Zack, could I?" he replied. "Which reminds me," he said to Poppy, "have you two got any energy left? The band's starting in a minute."

"Great!" said Poppy. "Come on, Zack," she said, "let's go and dance!"

"Finish your starter first, Poppy," said Mum, "or you'll be miles behind the rest of us. Once you get on that dance floor I'll never get you off again!"

Poppy ate her Dirty Dinosaurs, which was what Uncle Simon called her favourite starter, though it was really paté spread on bits of toast cut into dinosaur shapes. She really would have to tell him one of these days that she was getting a bit old for the dinosaurs, though she still loved the food!

The band was playing a cha-cha-cha. Some of the dancers around them could do this Latin American dance quite well, and some not at all. But everyone was having a good time, swaying to the "one, two, three-and-one, two, three" rhythm that Poppy and Zack knew so well.

"OK then, Pop," said Zack when they'd both finished eating. "Ready?" He took Poppy's hand and they swung into the cha-cha-cha. In class and at competitions Poppy danced with girls when there weren't enough boys to go round, but she always felt happiest dancing with Zack. It was hard not to think about next year, when she'd be dancing with someone else.

"It's weird doing a cha-cha-cha again," she said.

"I can't believe that in a week's time *Bugsy* will be finished," replied Zack.

"In Brighton, anyway," added Poppy.

By next Saturday, everyone's parents had to return the form to say whether or not their child could go to London to appear in the show there. It would mean being in London for three or four evenings a week for eight weeks – or possibly more, if the show was successful enough.

"Have your parents filled in your form yet?" asked Zack.

"No," replied Poppy. Earlier that day she had seen the blank form pinned to the noticeboard in the kitchen.

"Neither has my mum," said Zack.

As she and Zack did the turning-this-way-and-that step called the New York, Poppy saw Mum look at her and nudge Dad, who leaned over to say something to Tom. Tom spoke to Mrs Bishop and Auntie Jill, and everyone around the table smiled. When she was facing Zack again, Poppy said, "Look, they're all smiling at us."

"They must be plotting something," said Zack as the cha-cha-cha music ended and the band started to play something slower. "I know that look on my mum's face."

"Come on," said Poppy, pulling his hand, "let's go and find out what's going on."

"What are you all so pleased about?" asked Zack as they sat down.

Mrs Bishop glanced round the table, then leaned across to speak to Poppy. She wore an excited, hopeful expression. "Would you like to go to London?"

Poppy was puzzled. "I *am* going to London," she said. "When we move, in the summer."

"Trisha means, would you like to *dance* in London," said Mum, "in the show."

Zack's eyes grew very bright. "You bet!" he said.

"Well, you can," said Mum.

Poppy and Zack looked at each other in amazement. "*How?*" they asked, both together.

"Are we moving there *now?*" asked Poppy.

"Not exactly," said Dad, "at least, not into a new house. That won't be till the summer. But to make it easier for us to house-hunt, a friend of mine at work is letting us stay at a flat he's got in London. It's empty at the moment – it hasn't got anyone living there, or even any furniture. When we heard you and Zack had been asked to go to London, I phoned and asked him if he'd mind if you stayed there with me too, three nights a week for eight weeks." Dad's face broke into a grin. "And he said, no problem."

"Oh, Dad, that's fantastic!" cried Poppy.

"Thanks, Mr Love!" said Zack, his eyes almost popping out of his head.

"It'll be like camping out indoors," said Dad. "We'll have to sleep in sleeping bags and picnic on the floor."

The waiter arrived with their main courses. "Make the most of this delicious food," said Mum, laughing. "You'll have to put up with Dad's cooking in London, you know."

"I'm quite good at burnt sausages!" protested Dad.

Poppy couldn't decide if she was sad because she had to leave Brighton, or happy because she was going to London, or both. "I'm not dreaming, am I?" she asked Zack.

"No," said Zack, "but *two* surprises in one day – I'm flabbergasted!"

It was such a silly word, Poppy laughed. "I'm flabbergasted too!" she agreed.

"Camping out indoors sounds really fun," said Tom. "Can I come too?"

Everyone laughed. "If you can do the Charleston!" teased Dad.

As they were finishing their dinner, Uncle Simon appeared with two waiters. They poured champagne into the grown-ups' glasses and lemonade into the children's, but hesitated over Tom's. Dad nodded, and Tom grinned. "Excellent!" he said. "Champagne!"

Mum raised her glass. "Here's to the new house, and to Poppy and Zack's West End appearance!"

As the others raised their glasses, Auntie Jill, who had been quiet for a long time, suddenly spoke up. "Hold that toast, everyone. There's something else."

Auntie Jill took Uncle Simon's hand. "Zack said earlier that things change, and he's right.

There's going to be a big change in our lives. We're going to have a baby!"

Everyone was stunned for a moment, then they all started talking at once.

"To the house, the show and the new baby!" called out Dad.

There was a lot of hugging and handshaking, and then Auntie Jill came and gave Poppy an extra hug. "Goodness, Poppy," she said. "What a day of surprises!"

"This one's the best of all," said Poppy. "I'm going to have a cousin to dance with – and I can't wait!"

Natasha May loves dance of all kinds. When she was a little girl she dreamed of being a dancer, but also wanted to be a writer. "So writing about dancing is the best job in the world," she says. "And my daughter, who is a dancer, keeps me on my toes about the world of dance."

Shelagh McNicholas loves to draw people spinning around and dancing. Her passion began when her daughter, Molly, started baby ballet classes, "and as she perfected her dancing skills we would practise the jive, samba and quickstep all around the house!"